DORY
FANTASMAGORY
2 BOOKS IN 1!

Praise for

DORY
FaNTASMaGory
The Real True Friend

★"Well written, humorous, and engaging."
—*School Library Journal*, starred review

"Old friends and new will hope this highly successful sequel will not be the last starring this inventive, original child." —*Kirkus Reviews*

"Kids will find plenty to laugh about . . . A fine sequel to the popular series opener." —*Booklist*

"Lives up to and wonderfully expands the world of the original. It's genius."
—Travis Jonker, 100 Scope Notes Blog

"Dory is as likable a kid heroine as I've encountered in a decade." —*Boston Globe*

PUFFIN BOOKS
An imprint of Penguin Random House LLC, New York

Dory Fantasmagory first published in the United States of America by Dial Books for Young Readers, 2014
Published by Puffin Books, an imprint of Penguin Random House LLC, 2015

The Real True Friend first published in the United States of America by Dial Books for Young Readers, 2015
Published by Puffin Books, an imprint of Penguin Random House LLC, 2016

This omnibus edition published by Puffin Books, an imprint of Penguin Random House LLC, 2019

Visit us online at penguinrandomhouse.com

THE LIBRARY OF CONGRESS HAS CATALOGED THE DIAL EDITION OF DORY FANTASMAGORY AS FOLLOWS:
Hanlon, Abby, author.
Dory Fantasmagory / by Abby Hanlon
p. cm.
Summary: Dory, the youngest in her family, is a girl with a very active imagination, and
she spends the summer playing with her imaginary friend, pretending to be a dog,
battling monsters, and generally driving her family nuts.
ISBN 978-0-8037-4088-4 (hardcover)
1. Imagination—Juvenile fiction. 2. Imaginary companions—Juvenile fiction.
3. Brothers and sisters—Juvenile fiction. 4. Families—Juvenile fiction.
[1. Imagination—Fiction. 2. Imaginary playmates—Fiction. 3. Brothers and sisters—Fiction.
4. Family life—Fiction.] I. Title.
PZ7.H196359Do 2014 [Fic]—dc23 2013034996

THE LIBRARY OF CONGRESS HAS CATALOGED THE DIAL EDITION OF THE REAL TRUE FRIEND AS FOLLOWS:
Hanlon, Abby, author, illustrator.
Dory and the real true friend / by Abby Hanlon.
p. cm.
Summary: Dory, a highly imaginative youngest child, makes a new friend at school but her
brother and sister are sure Rosabelle is imaginary, just like all of Dory's other friends.
ISBN 978-0-525-42866-4 (hardcover)
[1. Imagination—Fiction. 2. Imaginary playmates—Fiction. 3. Schools—Fiction. 4. Friendship—Fiction.
5. Brothers and sisters—Fiction. 6. Family life—Fiction.] I. Title.
PZ7.H196359Dm 2015 [E]—dc23 2014034036

Dory Fantasmagory Puffin Books ISBN 9780147510679
The Real True Friend Puffin Books ISBN 9780147510686

This omnibus edition ISBN 9781984815279

Printed in the United States of America

1 3 5 7 9 10 8 6 4 2

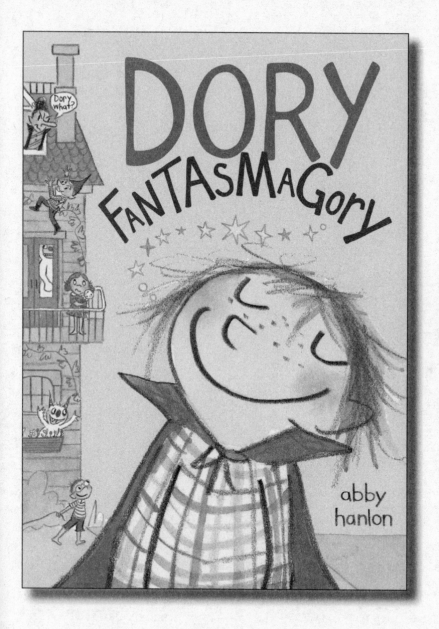

DORY
FaNTaSMaGory

abby hanlon

She's got imagination.

She's funny.
She's brave.

She's a dog.
No, she's a girl.

She's DORY—
what a rascal!

DORY
FaNTaSMaGory

abby hanlon

For Ann Tobias, my fairy godmother

FANTASMAGORY

a dream-like state where real life
and imagination are blurred together

CHAPTER 1
Such a Baby

My name is Dory, but everyone calls me Rascal. This is my family. I am the little kid.

My sister's name is Violet and my brother's name is Luke. Violet is the oldest. Violet and Luke never want to play with me. They say I'm a baby.

"Mom! Rascal is bothering us!"

"What is she doing?" calls my mother.

All summer long, whenever I try to play with Luke and Violet, they say, "PLEASE LEAVE

US ALONE!" Well, I'm not going to leave. But I can't think of what to say, so I ask questions. Any question I can think of.

"I can't wait for school to start so we can get a break from Rascal!" says Violet.

"Me too!" grumbles Luke.

"Don't talk about school!" I cover my ears. I never want summer to end. I like to stay home in my nightgown instead of getting dressed for school.

"It's a winter nightgown," says Violet.

"And it's inside out," says Luke.

"And it's backwards," says Violet.

"So what?" I say.

"So, now that you turned six, you need to stop acting like such a baby!"

"Why do you always call me a baby?" I complain.

"Because you talk to yourself," says Violet.

"And you have temper tantrums," says Luke.

"And you play with monsters," says Violet.

Talk to myself? I have no idea what they are talking about. I never talk to MYSELF. I talk to my friend Mary. No one can see her except me.

Mary *always* wants to play with me. She thinks I'm the greatest.

At night, Mary sleeps under my bed.

During the day, Mary follows me around. She wants to do whatever I'm doing. I usually don't mind, but sometimes I have to tell her no.

"Okay. Mary, what do you want to play?" I ask.

Here are some things Mary likes to do:

Try and steal Violet's doll, Cherry

fake sleep

Sneak cookies from
the high cabinet

exercise club

Get dragged around the
house in a laundry basket

Look for Monsters

The Toilet Monster   The Ketchup
                        Monster

The Vacuum
Monster

Mary is my favorite, but my house is actually
full of monsters. There is the Toilet Monster,
who comes into the bathroom if you sit on the
toilet for too long.

There is the
Ketchup Monster,
who makes weird
noises when you
squeeze the ketchup.
There is also the
Laundry Monster,

The Laundry Monster

The Living Room
Monster

The Broken Drawer
Monster

the Broken Drawer Monster, the Vacuum
Monster, the Upstairs Hallway
Monster, the Living
Room Monster,
and more.

Upstairs
Hallway
Monster

I try to warn Luke and Violet when I see one.

"Watch out! It's behind you!"

"AHHH! There's a monster in your underwear!"

"RUN! THE VACUUM
MONSTER IS COMING!"

But Luke and Violet don't appreciate it.

15

After dinner Violet and Luke say they have something important to tell me.

I follow them upstairs, skipping steps. I'm so excited. What can it be? Violet lets me sit on her bed. Maybe she will let me play with Cherry.

Very slowly Violet asks me, "Rascal, have you ever heard . . . of . . . someone named Mrs. Gobble Gracker?"

I shake my head no.

"Well, Mrs. Gobble Gracker is a robber, and she steals baby girls," says Violet.

"And she is five hundred and seven years old and has very sharp teeth!" adds Luke.

"And, well," says Violet, "you're going to be really surprised when I tell you this."

"What?" I say. I am dying to know.

"She's been looking for you," she says quickly.

"Are you serious?" I ask.

"Dead serious," she says.

"Mrs. Gobble Gracker is looking for *me*?" I ask in amazement.

"Shhhh," says Luke. "She's so scary you have

to whisper when you say her name, like this: *Mrs. Gobble Gracker . . ."*

"So, if I were you, I would stop acting like such a baby . . . so she doesn't come get you," says Violet. For a moment, I'm quiet.

This is a lot to think about. Luke and Violet stare at me, as if they are waiting for me to cry. "How will she get in the house? Does she come in the front door? Will she ring the doorbell?" I ask them.

Before they answer, I have some more questions, "Is she sneaky? Will I have to battle her? Does she wear a long black cape? Is it made out of fur? Is it real fur or fake fur? Are her teeth rotting? Does she brush them? Does she have a really creepy-looking nose? Does she have a cat? Does she live in a cave? Does she have really long bones?"

"WE DON'T KNOW! LEAVE US ALONE!" they shout, shaking their heads and walking away fast.

I follow Luke and Violet around the house.

"Oh my gosh! What have we done?" says Luke, covering his ears.

"This is the worst idea we have ever had," says Violet, trying to get away from me.

"Ever," says Luke. "Ever. Ever. Ever."

"I don't even want to know what happens next," says Violet.

CHAPTER 2
"Did You Hear the Doorbell Ring?"

The next morning I warn Mary. "Mrs. Gobble Gracker is five hundred and seven years old, and she has black teeth that are sharp like needles, and her pockets are full of dirty tissues. And ... she could be on her way over here right now, so don't act like a baby."

I've never seen a monster so scared.

Too tight.

When I hear
the doorbell, I run
downstairs.

"Okay! I'll get it," I say.

I run and hide under my parents' bed. There's something warm and furry under the bed. Someone is already hiding under this bed. It's Mary.

"Have you seen my cape?" I whisper. Mary reaches behind her and hands me my cape, all wrinkled up in a ball. She *always* takes my things and doesn't return them.

"I'm going to battle," I tell her as I put on my cape.

"Can I help?"

Nope. Too dangerous.

Then, as fast as I can, I run into Luke's room to look for his darts. But when I hear footsteps coming closer, I dive into his closet to hide.

It's dark and warm and kind of smelly. Actually, I'm very happy in the closet, so I decide to stay. Days and days go by, probably. I can hear my family saying, "Where's Rascal?"

"Heee, Heee! They'll never find me!" I giggle.

The footsteps again! OH NO! SHE'S GOING
TO FIND ME!

The closet door opens.

It's just boring old Luke!

"Rascal, what the heck are you doing in here?" he asks me.

"LEAVE ME ALONE!" I scream. I am so an-gry that he ruined my hiding spot.

"DON'T FIND ME. DON'T FIND ME!" I shout.

Then I kick and bang and throw some things. I cry so hard the room looks blurry and upside down.

After I'm done crying,
I feel all better. "Can I
borrow a dart?" I ask
Luke, drying
my tears.

"You're nuts," he says, and walks away,
which I think means yes.

I take the dart and run. In the hallway, I run
into Mary. She is pointing and jumping up and
down. "Mrs. Gobble Gracker went downstairs!
She's in the living room! What are you going to
do?" she yells.

"I'm going to shoot her with this special
sleeping dart. It will make her sleep for a hundred years."

"Wow!" says Mary. "That's a good idea."

"Don't follow me," I warn her.

There she is! Just sitting there! I hold my dart ready to shoot it across the room. Ready, one, two… Wait a minute. What did Violet just say?

"I'm the mommy and
you are the daddy," says Violet.

Are they playing house? I stop my battle.
I drop my dart. I want to play house.

"Now, we just need a baby," says Violet.

Baby????
Did somebody
say baby????

I CAN BE THE BABY!

My sister and
brother look at me
very carefully, trying
to decide. I show them
my cutest baby face. "Goo," I say.

Goo moo ga gee bu goo?

"Hhhhmmmm," says Luke.

"Wellllll . . ." says Violet.

"Hummmm," says Luke.

"I have a better idea!" says Violet, grabbing Cherry. "Cherry can be the baby!"

"Great idea," says Luke. "She's much quieter."

"And cuter," says Violet.

Stupid old baby Cherry,
I think. Using my scariest
voice, I clench
my teeth and
warn her, "Just
wait, one day
I'll get you."

43

As I walk away, I hold my head up high and think, I don't have time to play anyway. I'm *way* too busy.

But what *was* I so busy doing? I can't remember.

banana
peel

I know I was in the middle of something.

When I get back to my room, I snuggle in bed with my bunny. Then Mary comes in with my dart.

"Oh, yeah!" I say, "I was just about to shoot Mrs. . . . Uhhh . . . sshh . . . did you hear that?" Creaky sounds are coming from the stairs. Even the Upstairs Hallway Monster is scared and wants to hide out in my room. We peek out and see Mrs. Gobble Gracker looking angrier than before. It's time for me to be the brave one.

"Three, two, one . . ." I whisper.

And then I jump out and shoot my dart.

Mrs. Gobble Gracker stumbles around. She is walking into the wall, her knees are bending, her eyes are closing . . . she collapses! "I'll find that girl when I wake up," she mumbles, and then she is sound asleep.

I have to tell Luke and Violet! They should know that I shot Mrs. Gobble Gracker, because I was so quick and tricky and I had such good aim. They should know that no baby could do what I did. They should know!

I run to the living room and jump right on Violet's lap. I cup my hands around her ear.

I whisper my secret. "Mrs. Gobble Gracker is asleep in the upstairs hallway! I shot her with a sleeping dart! I'm dead serious."

"Mom! Rascal is bothering us!" calls Violet, pushing me off her lap.

"What is she doing?" calls my mother from the kitchen.

"She's spitting in my ear!"

"No, I'm not! I'm telling you a secret!" I shout.

But before my mother comes in the room, I run away as fast as I can. As I'm dashing up the stairs I hear my mom say, "Where did Rascal come up with this crazy Mrs. Gobble Gracker game?" I stop to listen.

"I have no idea," says Violet.

"How would *we* know?" says Luke.

Then I run down the hallway to my room, being careful not to trip on the body lying on the floor.

CHAPTER 3
Chickenbone

As I step over Mrs. Gobble Gracker's body on my way to breakfast, I start to worry. One hundred years *sounds* like a very long time, but what if one hundred years goes by really fast? I decide to wear my cow costume as a disguise just in case Mrs. Gobble Gracker wakes up. Just to be safe.

"Aren't you hot in that?" asks Luke.

"No. Yes. I don't want Mrs. Gobble Gracker to recognize me."

"Stop talking about Mrs. Gobble Gracker!" screams Violet.

"Stop talking about Mrs. Gobble Gracker!" I copy her.

While Mrs. Gobble Gracker is asleep, I finally have time to hang out with Luke and Violet.

I try and get Luke and Violet to laugh at me. Cereal time, I've discovered, is the best time for laughing. If I can get milk to come out of my nose, they always laugh. And if my parents sleep late, I can make them laugh by saying bathroom words.

But after cereal time, I have to work much
harder to get their attention.

"If you want, you can milk me," I offer Violet.

"Eeeew," says Violet.

"Okay, I'll milk myself and fill up a glass for
you," I offer.

"GET AWAY FROM ME!" screams Violet.

I follow Luke and Violet around the house and think of ways to impress them. Mary follows me.

"Can I draw a mustache on Mrs. Gobble Gracker while she is asleep?" asks Mary.

"No, that is way too risky!" I tell her.

"But she's snoring really loud!" says Mary.

"I'm busy," I say, waving her away.

"Hey, guys, do you want to see a magic trick? See the stick in this hand?" I say. Then I put my hands behind my back.

"Now it's in this hand. Ta-da!!"

"That's the worst trick I've ever seen," says Luke.

They didn't even want to see me eat a napkin.

"Hey, guys, do you know that I can sing without opening my mouth? I'm dead serious. Listen!"

"Can you please hum somewhere else?" says Luke.

"It's not humming, it's singing!" I say.

"Wait a minute . . . is that sweat?" says Violet, looking up. "Are you covered in sweat?" she asks. "Take that thing off!"

"Nope." I say, and fold my arms. "I will not."

"Why do you always have to act like such a baby?" asks Violet.

Then my mom yells:

I am boiling mad! "I was singing! You are interrupting!" I collapse onto the kitchen floor. The tile feels cool on my hot face. My tears fall onto the diamond patterns in the tile that I know so well from so many temper tantrums on the kitchen floor. As I'm screaming and kicking and crying, I unbutton my cow costume and strip down to my underwear because *it's way too hot to have this temper tantrum in a cow costume* . . . **not** because they told me to!

When I'm
all done, I put
my bathing
suit on and
go outside.

I find Mary asleep under a tree.

"Are you real sleeping or fake sleeping?" I ask her.

"Real sleeping," she says without opening her eyes. Now even Mary doesn't want to play.

I lie in the hammock all by myself and think maybe Luke and Violet are right. Maybe I am a baby. I think of all the babyish things I do: I still smell my bunny and suck my fingers to fall asleep. I still put my clothes on inside out. I still can't whistle. I still overflow everything I pour. I still want to wear my nightgown all day.

When I look up at the trees through my tears, I see someone up there looking down at me.

"Who are you?" I ask, rubbing my eyes, squinting into the sun.

"I'm your fairy godmother," says a little man, crawling down from the tree like a koala.

"Are you sure?" I ask. "You don't look like a fairy godmother."

"Well, pretty sure," he says, but he looks kind of confused to me. "Well, the important thing is, I'm here to help you." He says his name is Mr. Nuggy and that he lives in the woods.

"Boy, do I need help!" I say. "Can you turn me into something else? I have too many problems as a human."

"Sure," he says. "How about a pineapple?"

"Ummm. Okay," I say, shrugging. "Why not?"

He takes out his wand, "One! Two! Three! TA-DA!"

I look down at my body. "I don't feel like a pineapple," I say. "Do I look like one?"

Mr. Nuggy looks at me very carefully. He sniffs me. And pokes me. Then sadly he shakes his head no.

But then I have an idea. "How about a puppy?" I say. "Can you turn me into a puppy?"

"Definitely," he says, jumping up excitedly. "No problem at all!" He's lucky that I'm already really good at turning into a puppy.

"One, two, three." He waves his wand. I drop to my hands and knees.

"*Woof, woof, woof,*" I bark and wag my tail. Mr. Nuggy looks very pleased.

I turn into a puppy just in time . . .

"Where did that little girl go? She was just out here. And where did this stupid dog come from?" Mrs. Gobble Gracker asks Mr. Nuggy.

"You must be imagining things," says Mr. Nuggy. "There's no girl here."

"I know you're up to something, Nuggy," she says. "Your silly little tricks have never worked on me."

"Watch out," says Mr. Nuggy. "This dog bites."

I bark my head off at Mrs. Gobble Gracker.

"Somebody get this dog to shut up!" says Mrs. Gobble Gracker. She has absolutely no idea it's me!

Rrr– UFF!

"Woof, woof!" I say, which means, "My human days are over." *And boy, do I mean it.*

Mr. Nuggy says, "I have to go now. My wife needs me home for dinner." He starts to climb back up the same tree.

"Woof, woof, woof," I bark up the tree after him, which means, "Wait! What's your phone number?"

"You can call me from any banana," he calls down. "No numbers."

Then he disappears into the summer leaves.

Violet and Luke come outside to play Frisbee, and I run to tell them the news.

"I have great news! Mrs. Gobble Gracker will never find me."

"Really? You decided to stop acting like a baby?" asks Violet.

"No, I decided to stop acting like a human," I say.

"Oh brother," says Violet. "Don't tell me. I don't want to know."

"No problem," I say, "because I can't talk anyway. *Woof, woof.*

"*Woof, woofy, woof, woof,*" I say, chasing after the Frisbee.

"Beat it," says Violet.

But Luke says, "Come here, puppy." And he pets me.

"What's your name, puppy?"

I have to think of a VERY good name, so that Luke will be excited to play with me. I concentrate really hard.

Ooooooo, great hammock.

Finally ...

I say my name without really opening my mouth since puppies don't talk: "Chickenbone."

"Your name is *Chickenbone?*"

I nod my head yes and say, *"Woof, woof, woof."*

Luke looks pleased.

"Do you have an owner?" he asks.

I shake my head no, and make my saddest puppy eyes ever.

"Well," he says, petting me, "I could be your owner. But you have to be a good dog."

"Woof, woof, woof!!" I jump around and wag my tail and do somersaults to show how happy I am.

It turns out Luke really wants to be a dog owner. I never knew.

I have long shaggy white fur with brown

spots, and I have a pink polka-dotted bow, and a wet nose, and I'm very jumpy and I usually have spit on my face. Luke just can't get enough of me. He *loves* Chickenbone.

And that's how I became a dog named Chickenbone, and how Mrs. Gobble Gracker was left hanging around my house looking kind of bored and confused. I guess she is waiting for me to come back.

CHAPTER 4
If You Take a Dog to the Doctor

Luke puts my cereal bowl on the floor for me, and I hungrily eat it up. He gives me treats (which is more cereal) when I do my tricks. Here are my tricks:

lie down   spin   sit

Then I chase my dad
down the sidewalk as he
leaves for work.

Go
home,
dog.

Give me
my leg
back.

Err...

"*Woof, woof!*" I say, and jump on Violet, who
is still trying to get used to me. "Stop licking
me!!" she screams. "Gross!! Help!! Rascal is
licking me again!!!"

"Rascal, put
your tongue back
in your mouth!"
yells my mom.

At breakfast, I pick up socks with my mouth and bring them to my owner. I make my little puppy begging sounds until he throws the sock for me to fetch.

"I gotta go. Be a good little dog today," my owner says. I lie on my back so he can pet my belly. Luke and Violet are going to their friend's house. If I weren't a dog, I'd be really jealous.

Instead I'm so happy that I get to stay home all day and chew on socks with Mary.

But my mom surprises me with some terrible news: I have to get dressed.

"Put these on," says my mom, grabbing the socks from my mouth.

"*Woof, woof,*" I say, which means no.

"Rascal! We have to go! I'm not kidding!" she says. "You have an appointment at the doctor today. You have to have a checkup before you go back to school."

"*Woof, woof,*" I tell her, and shake my head no. I don't want to get dressed because I don't want to go anywhere.

I want to stay home in my nightgown, which is actually part of my fur.

"NOW!!!" yells my mom.

"Dogs don't get dressed. *Woof!*"

My mom says, "We are in a huge rush, let's go!" But no matter how many times she says it . . . "*Dory, did you hear me say we are in a rush??? We have an appointment. We can't be late*" . . . it just doesn't mean anything to me, *because I'm a dog!*

"A *woof-woof-woof-woof, woof . . . woof . . . a woof . . . woof, woof, woof*," I say, which means: "No thank you. I'm just going to stay home and chew on socks."

We are already on the sidewalk by the time
my mom finally gets my dress over my head.

I cry and have a huge fit, and people walk by
and stare at us.

Yuck, I hate this stupid dress. *Grrrrr.*

I had planned on changing back into a girl when we got to the doctor's office. But I discovered it became impossible to change out of being a dog. I was stuck as a dog and there was nothing I could do about it. These things just happen to me.

The doctor is very smiley. She asks me lots of questions.

"How old are you, Dory?"

"Woof, woof!" I say.

"What grade are you starting?"

"Woof!"

"Dory, you need to answer the doctor," says my mom, who looks embarrassed.

"I see you like to pretend you are a puppy. You are a very cute puppy," says the doctor. "What else do you like to do?"

"*Woof, woof, woof!*" I say.

"I'm so sorry," says my mom. "Dory is very imaginative, a little too imaginative."

"Wonderful," says the doctor, and she pets me. I want to lick her.

My mom whispers to me, "Put your tongue back in your mouth."

The doctor listens to my heartbeat, looks inside my ears, takes my blood pressure and my temperature, and makes my knees jump, and I am a good little puppy for all of it.

Then the doctor says she needs to check my eyes. She asks me to look at a chart, cover one eye, and say what letter she is pointing to. She points to an *E*.

"*Woof?*" I say.

My mom whispers, "Dory, if you don't say the letters, she's going to think you can't see them, and you are going to have to get glasses. *So you need to speak.*"

I imagine myself
wearing glasses and
it's very cute.

"What letter is this?"
asks the doctor pointing to an *F*.

"*Woof*?" I say.

My mom says, "I'm so sorry.
I know Dory can see just fine.
Maybe we'll have to do this
another day."

"Okay," says the doctor. "No problem. There's
just one more thing we need to do."

And right when I least expect it, just as the
doctor is saying what a *very healthy little puppy I
am* . . . she is holding a needle. I try to get away,
but I'm not fast enough. OOOOWWWW!!!! I
scream and cry.

1 Least expect it.

2. what's this?

3. Oh no!

4. Aaahhh!

5. Lollipops?

Then the doctor holds a basket of lollipops in front of me. "You can choose one lollipop for now, and one for later," says the doctor, smiling. My tears crawl right back into my eyes

94

when I see that basket of lollipops. I choose
one yellow lollipop for now, and just when the
doctor least expects it, I poke the lollipop stick
right in the doctor's thigh!!!

"Ouch!" she says.

"That's a shot for
you, too," I say.

"So you *can* talk,"
she says, smiling.

And then I make
my angry puppy face,
and growl. *"Gggrrr,"* I
say, showing her my
pointy teeth.

When it's time to go home, my mom puts my yellow lollipop in her purse and I know it's gone forever. I quickly put my shoes back on. My mom doesn't even have to ask me because I can tell by the way she is breathing that I should just do it.

On the way home, we pick up Luke and Violet at their friend's house. I quietly whimper like a dog to Luke so my mom can't hear. I raise my paws and make my eyes look droopy.

But my mom hears everything. *"Dory, that's it! I'm done! No more dog today!"* she snaps at me from the front seat.

I pout.

And for a few minutes, it's quiet in the car.

And then I whisper, "Who wants to hear how loud I can hum?"

CHAPTER 5
Time-out

When we get home from the doctor, I am in huge trouble. My mom tells me I have to go to my room for time-out. I say, "You can just leave my dog food in a bowl outside my door, *woof*!" This makes my mom so mad that she grabs my paw and drags me up the stairs.

"Walk!" she says.

"I am!" I cry.

"On two legs!!!" my mom yells.

Alone in my room, I suddenly don't feel like being a dog at all. I've got too many problems as a dog. I show Mary my wound. She feels so bad for me.

I put my nightgown back on and then I open my bedroom door a tiny bit. I can hear my family talking about me in the kitchen.

"Rascal gave the doctor a shot!" Luke says, laughing.

"She is out of control!" Violet says. She is laughing, too.

Then I hear an unfamiliar voice. "And she still got a lollipop?" says the voice. Who was that? It sounded like a wicked old . . . huuuuuuuh?!! Was that Mrs. Gobble Gracker? I do not believe it. I walk closer to the stairs to hear better.

"All she could do was bark. I've never been so embarrassed in my life!" says my mom.

"How babyish!" laughs the voice. Now I'm sure; it *is* Mrs. Gobble Gracker. Are they all sitting around the kitchen table together? And laughing at me? And it sounds like they're eating popcorn!

"Time-out is just what she needs," says my mom.

"I agree. Keep her locked up," grumbles Mrs. Gobble Gracker with her mouth full of popcorn.

I run back to my room to tell Mary. "Mrs. Gobble Gracker is downstairs *eating popcorn* with my family. *POPCORN!*"

"What's the big deal about popcorn?" asks Mary.

"She is eating popcorn with *my* family!" If Mary doesn't understand, I can't explain it!

"What are you going to do?" asks Mary.

"No more hiding! No more disguises! No more tricks!" I yell. "Something serious has to be done!"

"Like what?" she says.

"Give me that banana. I'm calling Mr. Nuggy!"

"Hello? Hi, it's me. Mrs. Gobble Gracker is eating popcorn with my family. Yes, I said popcorn . . . I can't believe it either, so can you please come back?"

Whoa, that was fast.

Mr. Nuggy crawls in the window and wipes his muddy boots.

"I've brought ingredients for a poison soup," he says. "This is how we get rid of Mrs. Gobble Gracker . . . permanently."

"What will happen when she eats the soup?" I ask.

"Well, first she will choke a little bit, and then feathers will come out of her ears, and then her eyeballs will turn into gloppy yogurt, and then she'll drop dead."

"Oh!" I say, hugging him. "You are the best fairy godmother in the world!"

But, something isn't quite right.

"I don't mean to be picky," I say, "but could you try and look *a little* more like a fairy godmother?"

"What do you have in my mind?" he asks.

I run to my closet to get some dress-up clothes.

Perfect.

Next, we make signs for the door because Mr. Nuggy says we need privacy to make our soup.

After we hang the signs, there's a knock on the door.

It's Luke. "Mom said you can come out of time-out now."

"No thanks," I say, and shut the door. Time-out is turning out to be *way* too much fun.

We don't want any more interruptions so we decide to send Mary out to be our spy. "Tell us if she's coming. And wear this wig!" I say, and give her a push out the door.

Now that it's quiet, Mr. Nuggy and I finally start cooking. We make the deadliest, most delicious poison soup for Mrs. Gobble Gracker's dinner.

When the soup is ready, we carry it down
to the kitchen, while Mary keeps Mrs. Gobble
Gracker distracted.

Then Mr. Nuggy and I gather materials for a giant fort where we can hide until dinnertime, while Mary keeps a look out.

We grab the blankets and sheets and pillows off the beds, and

collect all the rugs we can, and towels, and laundry, and bath mats, and put them in a big pile, surrounded by chairs. And we even have to move some tables, and put the chairs on the

tables, and we tie the whole thing up with a
huge roll of ribbon. And the amazing thing is
that we did this without my mom even notic-
ing because she is on the phone.

"Dinner is ready!" calls my mom from the kitchen. Of course, Mrs. Gobble Gracker is the first to arrive.

"Okay, now's your chance!" I tell Mr. Nuggy. "Go talk to her!"

From the fort, I can hear them in the kitchen.

"Good evening, Mrs. Gobble Gracker."

"Is that you, Nuggy? *Nice dress.*"

"Thank you."

"I have an important message from Dory. You remember Dory—the baby you were coming for. She has agreed to go with you. Back to your cave. Forever."

"Great because I almost forgot what I was doing here! Dory IS just what I wanted."

"But *after* dinner," he says.

"No problem," she says. "I'm starving."

Now that it's safe for me to leave my hiding spot, I come to the table for dinner. I sit next to Mrs. Gobble Gracker because I don't want to miss the moment when she chokes on her poison soup and drops dead. Hee. Hee. Hee. Mr. Nuggy and I make polite conversation.

"Do you like ice cream?" I ask Mrs. Gobble Gracker.

"I can't think of anything more disgusting," she says.

"Do you have a cell phone?" asks Mr. Nuggy.

"No, but I really really want one," she says. "Can you get me one?"

"Umm…?" says Mr. Nuggy, looking unsure what to say next.

"Do you have a cat?" I interrupt.

"I ate my cat," she says. "It was an accident."

"Oh, then I guess you aren't a vegetarian," I say.

"Yes," she says. "I would eat a vegetarian. Is that what we are having for dinner tonight?"

"We're having soup," says Mr. Nuggy. "Just soup."

Everything is going smoothly until my dad comes home from work and sits on Mrs. Gobble Gracker.

"It is?" says my dad, looking confused.

"You are sitting on Mrs. Gobble Gracker!" I tell him. "Can you please move??"

"It's been a loooooooooong day," says my mom to my dad.

At last everybody is at the table and sitting in their proper seat. Mr. Nuggy serves the soup. Mrs. Gobble Gracker picks up her spoon and tastes her soup.

"Delicious!!" says Mrs. Gobble Gracker, spooning more into her mouth as it drips down her chin. The soup is a disaster. Nothing happens. No feathers in her ears. No yogurt-y eyeballs. This is the end of me.

Mr. Nuggy whispers to me, "I'm so sorry. I must have forgotten an ingredient."

"Ouch!" screams Mrs. Gobble Gracker. Mary bit her ankle under the table.

"Thanks for trying, Mary," I say. But nothing can save me now.

Mrs. Gobble Gracker will probably bring me to her cave, I think, and put water in my cereal instead of milk and put me to bed too early, and not let me jump on her couch, and she won't take me to the library, and she'll eat all my Halloween candy, and she'll always forget to buy bubble bath, and she'll put soggy sandwiches in my lunchbox, and she'll say my nightgowns are too small and give them away to littler kids, and right when it's time to light my birthday candles, she won't be able to find matches . . . and . . . and . . . she might even cook me in a big pot!

"I'll miss you all," I tell my family. "I was such a great kid, and now I'm going to be taken away forever."

"Bye!" says Violet.

"So long!" says Luke.

As I'm being carried away, out of the corner of my eye, I notice baby Cherry in her cradle in the living room. Suddenly, I realize I don't need anyone's help. I can save myself.

I wiggle out of Mrs. Gobble Gracker's arms and run to pick up baby Cherry. I hold her up high so Mrs. Gobble Gracker can get a good look.

She stares at Cherry. And she stares at me. Then back to Cherry. Then back to me. I take a deep breath and try to look very grown up.

"Humph!" she says, grabbing Cherry from me. I open the door for her and just like that,

Mrs. Gobble Gracker walks
out the door with *stupid old
baby Cherry.*

Then I hear screaming.

It's my mom. She found my giant fort.

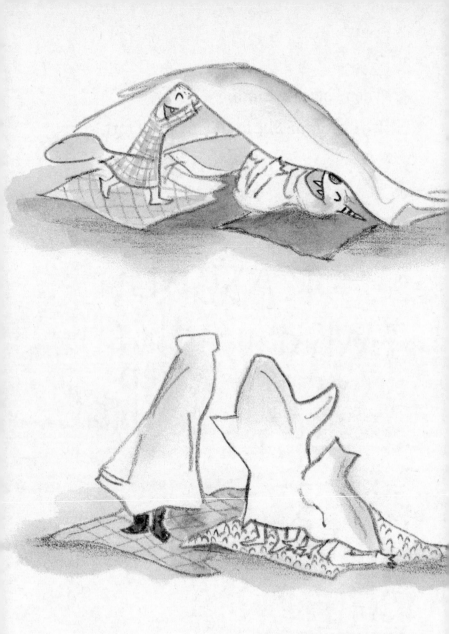

CHAPTER 6
Bouncy Ball

It takes a really long time to clean up the fort because I keep forgetting that I'm cleaning up.

"Rascal, bedtime!!!" calls my mom. "Brush your teeth!"

As I brush my teeth, I say good night to Mr. Nuggy. He has changed back into his regular clothes and is rushing home to see his wife.

That's when Violet bursts into the bathroom, crying. "I can't find Cherry anywhere!" she says. "And I've looked everywhere! She's gone!"

GULP

UH-OH. WHERE IS THAT DOLL?

"I'll be right back," I say.

I tiptoe downstairs and into the dark living room. *Oh! Where did I put Cherry?* I gave her to Mrs. Gobble Gracker, of course. But what did I REALLY ACTUALLY do with her? Think, think, think, I tell myself. I check all the usual places . . . the fridge, the toilet, the dishwasher, the garbage, under the couch,

in the couch,

under the rug,

upstairs . . .

In every drawer, under the beds, in the tub...

After looking everywhere, I found:

2 quarters

a silver button

a Hello Kitty eraser

a bunch of LEGOs

a moldy cookie

Cherry's shoe

Violet's rainbow bouncy ball

But no Cherry. I put the bouncy ball in my pocket.

I'm so tired! I give up. Cherry is definitely not in this house.

Well if she's not in this house, where is she? Did someone take her? But who would take her besides Mrs. . . . OH NO . . . Uuuuuhhhhhh!!

If Cherry is really gone forever, does that mean Mrs. Gobble Gracker IS REAL??

My dad hears my scream and comes running. "Why are you screaming like a maniac? You're going to wake up the whole neighborhood! Cut this out right now and go to bed!"

"AAAAAAAAAHHHHHHHHHHHHHH!"

He drags me by the arm. "We're done with you for the day, Rascal. Everybody is done with you, got it?"

"AAAAAAAAAHHHHHHHHHHHHHH!"

"Stop screaming!!" screams my dad.

"SHE WAS REAL!!!!" I scream.

"Okay, calm down, she was real, whatever you say," says my dad, dragging me down the hallway to my room. "Just go to bed."

Even my dad said she's real!

HELP!

"I have to be brave," I say, clinging to him.

"No! You have to go to bed!" he says, dropping me on my bed.

"Stay. In. Bed!" he says, pointing his finger at me. Then he tucks me in tight. "Because it's not safe for you to come out!" he says as he shuts my door, and I think I hear him laugh a tiny bit.

I fake sleep for a few minutes and then when I'm sure my dad is back downstairs, I sneak out of my room. I'm going to tell Violet the truth. That Cherry is gone forever and *it's all my fault.* And even though I know she'll want to kill me, she doesn't have to even bother. Because Mrs. Gobble Gracker is probably coming back for me.

I have an idea. After I tell her the bad news, I'll give Violet her old bouncy ball. That might make her feel *a little better.*

"Violet," I say quietly, clutching the bouncy ball tightly behind my back.

"What?" she says.

"There is something I have to tell you . . . um . . . I . . ."

But then, I don't believe what I see. My mouth drops open. *Is that Cherry?* Lying right there next to Violet? "How . . . how . . . how . . . did she get there?" I ask.

"Oh, Luke found her when he snuck outside to catch fireflies," says Violet. "I must've left her on the front stoop, but I don't know when."

"Oh," I say quietly. But inside my head, my thoughts are loud: OOOOOHHH!! The stoop!! Of course!! I threw her out the front door when Mrs. Gobble Gracker was leaving!

"What did you want to tell me?" Violet asks.

"Oh yeah, that . . . well . . ." I say, climbing into her bed and tucking myself into her cozy warm covers.

"Well, Mrs. Gobble Gracker isn't real after all," I say.

"I know. I'm the one who made her up, stupid."

"You did??? Oh yeah," I say. "Thanks, Violet, that was a fun game. But it got a little scary at the end."

I'm so happy that I get to stay home in this cozy little house with my family after all.

"Good night," I say to Violet.

"Good night," she says, giving me a little shove. "Now get into your own bed."

Before I get out of her bed,
I hide the rainbow bouncy ball
under Violet's pillow as
a secret little gift.

The next morning is Saturday and our parents are still asleep. Luke and Violet are playing with the bouncy ball that Violet found under her pillow.

They are laughing as the ball hits the ceiling and flies off the walls,
hitting them on
their heads.

"Let's bounce it on the stairs!" says Luke. On the stairs, they are laughing even harder.

Boy, do I wish I could play.

Suddenly it's quiet. I run upstairs to go look.

The bouncy ball . . . bounced into the toilet.
Luke and Violet stand over the toilet staring
down at the sunken ball.

"What should we do?" shrieks Violet.
"Are we in trouble?" asks Luke.

"We'll have to get it out," says Violet.

"How do we do that?" asks Luke.

And then they both turn around to find me behind them, watching. Smiling.

"Rascal will get it, right, Rascal?" says Violet, nodding her head yes.

Right away, I roll up my nightgown sleeve and I stick my arm deep into the bottom of the toilet.

Luke and Violet cringe and cover their eyes and make gagging noises.

"Here it is!" I say, holding up the bouncy ball, my arm dripping toilet water.

Violet squeezes practically the whole bottle of foamy soap on my arm and helps me wash my hands and the ball. "Thanks, Rascal," says Violet. "You saved the bouncy ball!" I am so happy. I am beaming! We all agree that we don't need to tell Mom and Dad.

All day, all I can think about is the bouncy ball. Every time I think about it, I feel so proud. "Remember when I saved the bouncy ball?" I ask Violet.

"Uh-huh," she says.

After dinner Luke says, "Rascal, close your eyes and open your hand."

My whole life I've always wanted someone to say this to me.

Before I even open my eyes, I know exactly what it is: It's the rainbow bouncy ball.

"You can *borrow* it, Rascal," Violet says. "It's not to keep!"

"Really?" I say. *"Really???"*

"Since you saved it," she says.

I hug Luke and Violet.

"Let's play!" says Luke.

"Yeah!" says Violet. "Bounce it!"

I try and think of the best bouncy ball game I can think of. I hold the bouncy ball very tightly, close my eyes, and concentrate.

All these pictures come
rushing into my brain
at once.

"Okay, I got it! The ball is really a poison gum ball, and if it hits the ceiling, it explodes, and hot lava pours out of it, and we all melt. And when we melt, we turn back into cavemen, and Mrs. Gobble Gracker lives in the cave next door and she . . ."

"No! Not Mrs. Gobble Gracker *again!*" says Violet.

"Okay," I say, " but everything else?"

They agree. "Okay, everything else," they say.

My brother and my sister and I play bouncy ball. I run like a maniac to catch the ball, running into the walls, and screaming as it bonks me in the head. When the ball hits the ceiling we explode! I'm jumping up and down and making loud crashing sounds, the kind of sounds the earth makes when it blows up.

I leap onto Luke to protect myself from the hot lava. Hot lava is spilling all over the floor! It's bubbling everywhere! We jump on the couch, and move the pillows around so that we have a secret cave.

Now we are cave people!

Violet is the cave mommy, of course, and Luke is the caveman daddy hunter, and guess who gets to be the cave baby? ME! And I'm *the cutest* little cave baby.

THE END

DORY FANTASMAGORY

The Real True Friend

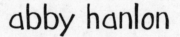

abby hanlon

To my collaborators

Louisiana   Burke

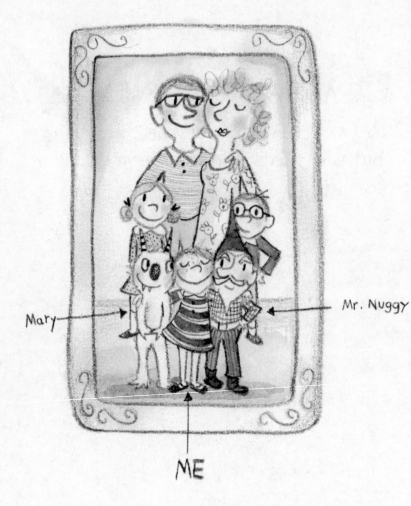

Mary

Mr. Nuggy

ME

CHAPTER 1
Such a Weirdo

My name is Dory, but everyone calls me Rascal. This is my family.

I have a mom, dad, big brother, and big sister who are just regular people. I also have a monster and fairy godmother who are not regular because only I can see them.

Mary is my monster. She sleeps under my bed and plays with me all day. Mr. Nuggy is my fairy godmother. He lives in the woods but comes over if I have an emergency. And I'm about to have an emergency pretty soon because . . .

1

... tomorrow is the first day of school!

I tell Mary the big news while we are playing our favorite game, exercise club.

Wait. What is school again?

"Oh yeah. Oh yeah. That place! With the water fountains!" says Mary. "There are so many kids and not a lot of grown-ups! Yippee! I love that place!" she says. "Let's get packing!"

Mary decides to make a list of what I should bring.

"I'm sorry, but I *cannot* read this," I say.

So she reads it to me. "Please bring to school tomorrow: Your dad's dirty laundry, extra salami, and lemon juice."

"*What a weird list!*" I say. "Are you *sure* you remember what school is?"

"Uh-huh. Super sure," she says.

"All right," I say. "I'm trusting you."

First, we collect
as much of my dad's
dirty laundry as we
can.

Then I stuff the laundry in my backpack. It makes me look like a big kid with a backpack full of home-work. *So that's what it's for!*

Second, we sneak down to the kitchen. Luckily, no one is there. I grab a handful of salami and put it in my lunch box. It's true, my mom never packs me enough salami!

Third, we look for
the lemon juice.

"Okay. Let's figure out what this
is for," I tell Mary. "I'm gonna
take a tiny squeeze, and you
tell me what happens."
WOW! OOOO-YA!

"So?" I ask.

"Your muscles are HUGE!" says Mary.

"What else?" I say.

"And your bones are lit up like lightbulbs!"

"What else?"

"And you have magic eyebrows!" says Mary.

I don't know what that means, but I like it.

"Let's pack it!" I say.

Just then my brother and sister come in the kitchen.

"What are you doing?" asks my sister, Violet.

"Nothing," I say, while Mary quickly sneaks the bottle of lemon juice into my lunch box.

"You know, Rascal, you're going to have to get *dressed* for school! You can't wear that dirty old nightgown every day anymore," says Violet.

"And you can't talk to yourself at school," says my brother, Luke.

"And do not move the furniture around in your classroom to build a fort like you did last year," says Violet.

"Just try not to imagine things!" says Luke. "That's ALL you have to remember, Rascal."

"Right," says Violet, pointing her finger. "No matter what, do NOT use your imagination!"

". . . like telling people that monsters live in our house!" says Luke.

". . . or talking about Mrs. Gobble Gracker!" says Violet.

"*Mrs. Who?* I'm done with her!" I say, which is a huge lie because Mrs. Gobble Gracker is still my favorite game.

Mrs. Gobble Gracker is a robber, and she is five hundred and seven years old, and she has very sharp teeth, and she wanted to steal me away from my family and lock me in her cave forever, but I was too tricky.

"And," says Violet, "the most important thing for you to remember is, DON'T BE YOURSELF. Can you do that?"

"Rascal? What are you staring at?" says Luke. "Pay attention!"

"Do you know why we are telling you all this?" says Violet, shaking my shoulders. "Wake up! Pay attention!

12

"BECAUSE!! IF YOU ACT LIKE SUCH A WEIRDO, NOBODY WILL WANT TO BE FRIENDS WITH YOU."

Violet's words are like giant rocks that fall from the sky and hit me on my head one by one and make the monsters disappear.

"What?" I say.

Violet says slowly, "Because. You. Won't. Have. Any. Friends."

"I don't care," I say. But I imagine myself all alone at recess.

"If you want friends," says Violet, "you should listen to me. You should plan your outfit for the first day of school."

"I'm busy already," I say, walking backward out of the kitchen. Then I turn around and run upstairs to my room and shut the door.

As fast as I can, I take all of my clothes out of my drawers, every single one of them, and put them in a big huge pile so that I can plan my outfit for tomorrow.

I search for all my best clothes to wear on the first day of school.

These plaid pants

 This polka-dotted shirt

This...  rainbow shirt on top

 striped socks

Santa hat...no....yes ...no... I can't decide....

"Definitely wear the hat!" says Mary.

"That's what I thought," I say.

She looks amazing.

"But what am *I* going to wear to school?" asks Mary.

Last year, I brought Mary to school with me every day. But now I think she'd better stay home. Especially when I remember last year . . .

LAST YEAR:

Mary always said she had to go to the bathroom, when she really didn't have to go. She just wanted to play with the soap in the bathroom. So one day the teacher said NO she couldn't go. But guess what? She really did have to go! So do you know what happened? ... *All over the floor.*

Also, it turned out that Mary was hiding salami in her desk.

What on earth is that smell?

Oh yeah, and one day she took her shoes off and then she couldn't find them. . . . Nobody *ever* found them. I felt so bad for her that I let her borrow my shoes.

She also whispered bathroom words in everybody's ears.

And she could never remember to raise her hand. She interrupted all the time. And her answer for everything was "chicken!"

> What word rhymes with house?

> Chicken.

"Sorry, Mary, you have to stay home," I tell her. "Last year was too crazy!"

Mary sulks. "But without me, you won't have a friend."

"I'm going to make a new friend," I say. "A *real* friend."

"NOOOOOOOO!!!" says Mary, bursting into tears, "Pleeeeease, no!!!"

That night my brain keeps waking me up with so many questions.

I wake up my dad
and tell him I have a
stomachache.

He says, "You don't really have a stomachache." And I say, "But how do you know?" And
he says, "Because the other night you told me
you had a stomachache in your ear."

"So?" I say.

"Good night!" he says.

But I still can't sleep, so I call Mr. Nuggy.

Whoa,
that was fast.

"I'm scared about school," I say. "I don't want to go. You've got to help me. What can you do? Can you use your magic wand to make it go away?"

"Don't worry," he says. "I have a plan. I'm going to do some magic and turn your whole school into a pancake, so you won't have to go, ever."

"A pancake?" I ask.

"Yes, but it's a very complicated recipe, and I'm going to need some chickens, and it might take a few days."

"All right, that's okay," I say.

A pancake sounds just fine, I think. *A great big giant buttery pancake instead of school would be perfect* is my last thought before I close my eyes and finally fall asleep.

CHAPTER 2
Best Friends Forever

When I come down for breakfast, Violet bursts out laughing. "Mom! Rascal is wearing the exact same outfit she wore every day last year! And now it's way too small for her!"

My mom says, "Oh, she can wear what she wants. It's not a big deal."

"The Santa hat isn't too small," I say.

"*But it's a Santa hat!*" yells Violet.

While I'm eating breakfast, my mom sits

down with me and says she has some important reminders about school.

1. "Don't move the chairs and desks around the room."

"I ALREADY KNOW ABOUT THAT!" I yell.

"Okay, okay, calm down!" she says.

2. "Keep your shoes on."

"Why would I take my shoes off?"

"I don't know, Dory. I still don't understand how you lost so many shoes last year."

3. "Absolutely no bathroom words! Do you understand me, Dory? I mean it. Save them for home, when you are in the bathroom, all by yourself, with the door shut."

"BOR–ING!" I say.

"I think you are going to have a super day," says my mom. "I'll miss you."

Why is mom not saying anything about the Santa hat?

As we leave for school, Luke says, "We are not walking with you if you wear that hat."

"Oh, fine," I grumble.

When we get to school, Violet walks me to my classroom door. I grab on tightly to her. I wish I were home in my nightgown.

"Don't leave me here," I say. But she is already walking away.

The teacher meets me at the door and says, "Let's hang up that *huge* backpack," and she walks me to the closet, smiling. I immediately fall in love with the closet.

It's sooooooo long! It has six doors! There are no cubbies like last year, so you can crawl

around. I hang up my backpack on a hook. I want to sneak right into that dark cozy space behind all the backpacks, but the teacher is standing there waiting for me.

"Now let's find your table," she says.

There is somebody at my table who is stuck in a shirt.

I'm stuck! I'm stuck! HELP!

I look around for the teacher to help, but she is already helping someone else.

Oh dear. I'm going to have to do this. I pull really hard on his shirt, and pull and pull and pull, and off it comes! *It's George!* George was in my class last year. "Thanks," he says, and then he falls off his chair.

When he gets up, he asks me, "Where's Mary? Did you bring her?"

"No," I say, embarrassed that he remembers.

"Aw shucks!" he says. "She was so funny. I liked when she moved all the furniture around."

I pretend that I have no idea what he is talking about.

The teacher gives us markers and tells us to draw self-portraits. I draw myself as a dog named Chickenbone. I give myself an eye patch, just 'cause. George draws himself with a bunch of creepy scars on his face.

I peek at the drawing of the girl sitting next to me. What???? OH MY!

She drew earrings! And earlobes! And curly eyelashes! And nostrils!! And a crown—covered in jewels!

When I look at her, she smiles at me, oh my . . . Holy Cow! I don't believe it . . . *SHE IS MISSING HER TWO FRONT TEETH!!!*

I decide at that very moment that she is my best friend.

She is wearing an old-fashioned dress that looks especially poufy. She has sparkly shoes with little tiny heels. She wore heels! *To school!* She smells like bubble bath, and she even has circle earrings that I think she drew on with a green marker. And I don't know why, but she is wearing her headband on her forehead instead of her head.

I decide to whisper something funny to her. "Do you know what happens if you don't put the tops back on Magic Markers?" I say.
She shakes her head no.

"They EXPLODE! *POW! BOOM! WHAM!*" I say.

I thought she was going to laugh, but in-stead she looks worried and quickly puts all the tops back on the markers.

But George gets excited by this and he explodes—"POW! BOOM! WHAM!"—and falls out of his chair again.

"That was fun," says George, lying on the floor, looking dizzy. That's what he always says when he gets hurt. Even if he is crying, he still says it. Then he leans forward and points to the girl. "Your forehead is falling down!" he says to her.

"What?" she says, grabbing on to her forehead.

"He means your headband," I say.

"It's not a headband," she says, and keeps drawing.

And then I hear her mumble in a very quiet whisper, "It's a crown."

George and I look at each other, confused.

At story time
on the rug, I rush
to get a seat next
to her.

The teacher says to her, "Rosabelle, move over a little please."

ROSABELLE? Did she say Rosabelle?? That is the most beautiful name *I have ever heard in my entire life. Rosabelle, Rosabelle, Rosabelle* I say in my head over and over again.

At lunchtime, I sit next to Rosabelle and George sits next to me. We watch in amazement as Rosabelle opens her lunch box, and takes out first a flowered place mat and matching cloth napkin (which she places on her lap), then a matching china cup and saucer. Then she takes out her water bottle and pours water into the cup and takes a little sip with her pinkie sticking up in the air like this:

Then she takes out a peanut butter and jelly sandwich and cuts it up with a knife and takes bites with a fork, while wiping her face with the napkin after each bite. I am so busy watching Rosabelle eat that I barely have time to eat my salami.

When it's finally recess, I get my first chance to be alone with Rosabelle.

"How did you get so poufy?" I ask Rosabelle, pointing to her dress.

She looks down and says, "It's a secret, but I'll show you."

Underneath her dress, she has six different skirts on. She shows me each one. And for each one, I say, "Wow!"

1. One flower skirt

2. One plaid skirt

3. One strawberry skirt

4. One polka-dotted skirt

5. One palm tree skirt

6. One very ruffly skirt

"Guess what?" I say. "I have a secret, too."

"You do? What is it?" she asks.

I'm trying to think of a secret. . . . I'm sure I have one. . . . I usually do.

I unzip my lunch box and take out the lemon juice. "It's a magical liquid. Do you know what happens if you squeeze it into your mouth? You get very strong and you can fight bullies!"

Rosabelle looks really surprised.

"Are there bullies???" she asks. "Are they dangerous?"

"I don't know yet . . . but watch me try it. . . ." I squeeze some in my mouth, but I get WAY too much, a huge enormous gulp. It's SOOO sour, I can't help but make a *really crazy face,* and I start choking and gagging.

"Are you all right?" she asks.

I nod my head yes, but I'm still gagging.

Just then some girls run toward us, giggling
and screaming, saying, "Rosabelle! Hopscotch!
Hopscotch!" And they
pull her away.

In the afternoon, we have choice time. When everyone is busy, I sneak into the closet for a super-quick bite of salami.

This is heaven.

It's so good that I stuff some salami in my pockets, so I can share with Rosabelle.

"Here . . . look, do you want some floppy cookies?" I whisper to her, which is my nickname for salami because I love it so much.

She does not.

After school, we line up to wait for our parents. My mom comes first.

She holds my hand and we walk toward the school yard gate. But a few steps away, I realize, I just have to tell Rosabelle. *I just have to.*

"BEST FRIENDS FOREVER!!!" I shout, jumping up and down.
She smiles.

BEST FRIENDS FOREVER!

My mom says to me, "Really? You have a best friend already?"

"Yes, I do! I do! A real true friend!"

"What is her name?"

"Um???"

Oh gosh . . . *what was her name?* Something beautiful, but I JUST forgot it. Was it Anna-belle? Rosebud? Roseblossom?

"Oh, I don't remember," I say. "What's my best friend's name again?"

CHAPTER 3
Chicken Soup

By the time I get home from school, Rosabelle's name has popped right back into my head. This time it stays forever.

"Did you hear about my best friend Rosabelle?" I ask Luke and Violet.

"About ten times already," says Violet.

"Well, she's extremely poufy. And she doesn't have a lot of teeth. And she wears a crown!"

"Not another monster!" says Luke.

"Forget it," I say angrily.

I wait until he walks away and then I jump
on top of him.

"Rascal!" he yells,
but then laughs ...
because it was such a
good surprise attack.

And then we wrestle,
and then he drags me
around on the floor ...
my favorite.

When Luke gets bored playing with me, I go upstairs to my room. I open the door and I am shocked. The floor is covered in paper. It looks like Mary's been making rows and rows of letters *all day*.

"I'm practicing the alphabet! Look at these *s*'s! See how good I would be at school? Don't you think you should bring me?" she says, holding up pages and pages of *s*'s.

"I love my *s*'s so much, I'm going to save them to show my children one day."

"I'm not sure . . . ," I tell her, "but I think those *s*'s are all backward."

She falls over in disappointment.

"Come on, get up," I say. "Stop moping around. What else happened today while I was gone?"

"I played school with all the monsters. I was the teacher!"

"No wonder it's such a mess in here," I say.
"They listened to you?" I ask her.

"Mostly," she says.

"Okay, what else happened?" I ask her.

"Mr. Nuggy called lots of times," she says.

"Mr. Nuggy *called me?* That's not how it's supposed to go! I'm supposed to call him! He's MY fairy godmother," I say.

"Well, he said he had an emergency."

"What kind of emergency could he have? *I'm the one with emergencies!*"

"I don't know, I couldn't understand him. He was bokking."

"*Bokking?* What the heck does that mean?"

Bokking?

"And it sounded like bokking from a cave or something. There was an echo."

"A *cave??*" Why would he be in a cave? "Quick, give me a banana."

"It's ringing. . . . Shh. . . . Hello?"

"*DoryDoryDory* . . . ," says an evil voice. "I knew you would call." I'd recognize that voice anywhere.

"Mrs. Gobble Gracker?! Why do you have Mr. Nuggy's phone? Where is he?" I shout.

"Well . . . I ran into him in the woods the other day. He was trying to do some magic helping YOU, I guess, but he accidentally turned himself into a chicken. Now he's stuck. YOU KNOW how that happens. Well, I have some water boiling . . . it is getting to be dinnertime, and YOU KNOW how much I love soup . . . chicken soup."

"Mr. Nuggy is a chicken?" I scream into the phone.

"OH NOOOOOO! HE'S NEVER GOING TO BE ABLE TO TURN MY SCHOOL INTO A PANCAKE NOW! *DON'T EAT MY FAIRY GODMOTHER!*"

"What are you doing?" Violet suddenly appears in my doorway. "Please tell me you aren't playing Mrs. *Gobble Gracker*," she says.

"I'm in the middle of an important call," I tell Violet in my dead serious voice.

"Okay, fine," she says, turning away. "I guess you don't want to talk about school . . . or Rosabelle."

"Wait, I do," I say, and drop the banana.

"So, did you play with Rosabelle at recess?" she asks.

"Uh-huh," I say, even though it's not true. "It was really fun."

"What did you guys play?" she asks.

"We played . . . um . . . Mermaid . . . Puppies," I say the first two words that pop into my head.

"Mermaid Puppies . . . " she says. "Huh."

Maybe Violet has a feeling that I'm not telling the truth, because then she says, "You should plan your outfit for tomorrow. Wear something that Rosabelle will like."

"Okay, good idea," I say.

As soon as Violet leaves, I pick up the banana again. This time I whisper. "Hello, are you still there? Sorry to keep you waiting."

"It was very rude," says Mrs. Gobble Gracker.

"I'm sorry, I couldn't help it."

"What are Mermaid Puppies?" she asks.

"What? You could hear that? I don't know what Mermaid Puppies are! That's not the point of this conversation! Listen, please don't eat Mr. Nuggy. I beg you. I'll give you anything. Just tell me, *what do you want?*"

"I'll think about it," she says. "I'll let you know."

"*When?*" I say. "I need to know when!"

But she has already hung up.

Without Mr. Nuggy, I'm on my own. And now Mary is so jealous of Rosabelle, she is having a fit.

And look! I'm missing teeth, too. What's the big deal about that?

I don't care that she can draw nostrils.

I hope she trips in her stupid, tiny heels!

So I have nothing left to do but wait for Mrs. Gobble Gracker to call back. And plan my outfit . . .

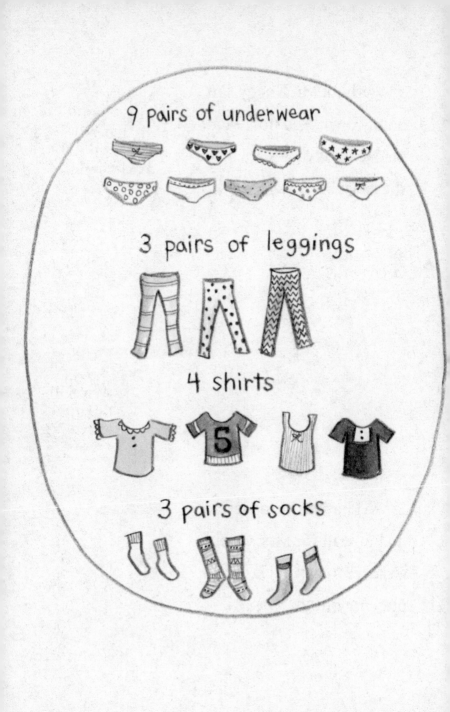

CHAPTER 4
Get Out of the Sticky Frogs!

The next morning, I wake up early because I need time to put on my outfit.

When I come down for breakfast, Violet says, "Why do you look weird?"

"No, I don't," I say, deciding it would be better not to tell her.

"You look . . . all bunchy," she says.

"And your butt looks big," says Luke.

"And you're sweating," says Violet.

"I don't know what you are talking about," I lie.

When I get to school, I tell Rosabelle, "Just wait till recess, I have a new secret for you."

"Is it recess yet?" I ask my teacher.

"No, honey," she says. "We just got here. Come to the rug for circle time."

During circle time, I have to wait forever and forever for my turn to speak. *Everyone in this class has something to say!*

I wait and wait for my turn to speak, and while I'm waiting I'm imagining that all the kids on the rug are newborn hamsters.

I snap out of it when it's Rosabelle's turn.

"Your stuffed animal?" says the teacher. "How cute."

"NO," says Rosabelle, shaking her head with a frown and then staring at the teacher as if the teacher is totally crazy. After a long silence, she says, "He flew into a hedge of thorns trying to save me."

Dragon??? Hedge of thorns? What is she talking about??

"Oh? Okay," says the teacher. "Very cute. Moving on . . . Dory, what did you want to say?"

"Um . . . um . . . ," *Of course, now I forgot.*

"That's okay, just tell us when you remember," says the teacher.

But there is no way I am going to lose my turn to speak! So I say the first thing I can think of. "I have a great game we could play today!"

73

"Can we pretend that all the kids are baby hamsters and you are trying to catch us and put us in a suitcase?"

My teacher says, "Uhhhh. . . . That sounds like a very fun game you could play at recess today, Dory."

"Well, if Rosabelle wants to . . . ," I say, looking at her.

But she doesn't look like she wants to.

The teacher smiles and says, "Does anybody
else have something to share this morning?"

George raises his hand and says, "I would
like to be a baby hamster named Marvin."

At lunch I can barely talk to Rosabelle because George won't stop talking about the hamster game. "Let's be hamsters with really bad manners! And we eat garbage! And we are hiding from the police! The police want to

capture all the hamsters and sell us to make hamster burgers! Raise your hand if you hate hamster burgers!" George says raising his hand.

"Gross!" I say, but it does sound kind of fun.

Finally it's recess.

"Ready for my secret?" I say to Rosabelle. I show her my nine pairs of underwear, three pairs of leggings, four shirts, and three pairs of socks.

"Now we are like twins!" I say. "We both have secret clothes!"

"Hmmm . . . ," she says, studying me carefully. "So you're padded. . . . Is it for protection? Is it like armor?"

I don't know how to answer that. "Well, it could be."

"Rosabelle! Come on!" The hopscotch girls are calling again.

"They were in my class last year," she says to me before they pull her away.

I take off three sweaty shirts. Then I follow her to the hopscotch game.

"Be careful!" I yell. "That
square is full of dead sharks!
Don't jump on the dead sharks!"

Rosabelle jumps to the
next square. "Holy moly!
Now you are stepping
in sticky frogs! *Get out of
the sticky frogs!*" Rosabelle
loses her balance and
lands in another square.

"AHHH!! Bubbling
hot lava!! Jump out!
Jump out! Quick!" I yell.

All the girls stop and look at me.

They keep looking at me.

"Do you want to play?" one of the girls asks me.

"Not really," I say. And I run away.

I wander around the school yard and watch what everyone else is playing.

There are girls galloping like horses.

There are kids playing house, but their house burned down and now they are all fighting.

George and some kids are playing hamsters.

Mary is doing her exercises.

Mary???!! What is she doing here?? I stomp over to her. "What are you doing here?" I ask angrily.

"Don't you want to exercise?" she says.

"Okay, just this once," I say. "But then go home!"

CHAPTER 5
Ring, Ring, Ring!

That afternoon, we have drawing time. Instead of starting my picture, I watch what Rosabelle draws. A big huge scaly dragon.

"Do you really have a dragon?" I ask her.

"Of course, I do," she says. "He's such a baby, though, and he always gets hurt. He even bumps into walls in the castle."

"You live in a castle?" I ask her.

"Where else would I live?" she asks. "Although I do have a little cottage in the woods when I need to hide."

"Do you have an underground base? I do!" says George. "Raise your hand if you have an underground hamster base!" he says, raising his hand.

I ignore George and ask Rosabelle, *"Hide from what?"*

"You know… creepy old witches, that kind of thing," says Rosabelle.

"Dory, aren't you going to draw something?"
asks the teacher, looking at my blank paper.

"Dory," she says, "can you hear me?

"Dory . . . ? Are you
there, Dory . . . ?"

After school, I rush straight to my room to get all my layers off and put my nightgown on and find out if I got any phone calls while I was gone.

"*She didn't call yet?*" I say. "Ugh! And I already told you! You don't have to raise your hand at home!"

Mary wants to come to school with me so

badly that she's been raising her hand whenever she wants to speak.

All afternoon, she won't stop practicing for school.

She is quiet in the hallways.

She even waits in line for the bathroom.

Since Mary is driving me crazy, I'm happy when Luke and Violet finally come home from their friend's house.

"Guess what? I have *BIG HUMONGOUS NEWS!*" I tell them. "Rosabelle has a dragon! And she lives in a castle! I'm dead serious."

"See," Luke says to Violet. "I told you Rascal made Rosabelle up."

"What? I did not make her up! She is a real girl in my class! She sits next to me!"

"Is she real in the same way Mary is real?" asks Violet.

"Yes!" I say.

Mary smiles proudly.

"What does your teacher say when you talk to Rosabelle at school?" asks Luke.

"She says, '*Girls, please be quiet!*'"

Luke laughs at this.

"Do you play with anyone else at recess besides Rosabelle?" asks Violet.

"Well, I only play with Rosabelle sort of because she mostly likes to play hopscotch," I admit.

"Your imaginary friend doesn't even want to play with you!" Luke bursts out laughing again.

"I ALREADY TOLD YOU!!! ROSABELLE IS NOT IMAGINARY!!!!" I scream at the top of my lungs.

As I stomp out of the room in tears, Luke and Violet are still laughing. I hear Violet say, "Well, she told me they play *Mermaid Puppies.*" Then I hear a loud thud. Luke must have laughed so hard he rolled off the couch. Like *Mermaid Puppies* is the funniest thing they've ever heard in their life.

I cry so hard that my whole room fills up with tears. Why are Luke and Violet such jerks? And what is so great about hopscotch? Will Rosabelle ever play with me? And where is Mr. Nuggy when I need him most?

"Maybe Rosabelle isn't my real true friend after all," I cry to Mary. "Maybe I'll never have a friend. Maybe Luke and Violet are right."

Mary pets my head while I cry.

"You can come to school with me tomorrow," I say, sobbing and sniffling.

"No thanks," she says.

"*WHAT?*" I say.

"I think I like *playing* school better than actually going."

"Ma-rrrrry! After all that begging? Errrr. But I need you now. I have no one to play with," I cry.

"I bet tomorrow Rosabelle will play with you," she says.

"How do you know?" I ask.

"*Just be yourself,*" she says.

So that's what I do.

The next day at lunch, I sit next to Rosabelle. It's not easy to get a seat next to her, with the hopscotch girls around.

I open my lunch box and I AM SHOCKED to discover that my mom packed *my phone!!* Why would she pack my phone? *What was she thinking?* Oh my goodness, *WHAT IF IT RINGS?*

Please please *please*
don't let it ring.
Uh-oh.

RRINNG RRRING RRING!

I have to answer it.

If I don't answer it, Mr.

Nuggy will be chicken soup.

"Hello?"

"Dory, how are you?" asks Mrs. Gobble
Gracker.

"Fine," I say, looking around the noisy cafe-
teria. I have to cover the other ear so I can hear
her.

"I've decided what I want," she says.

"It's about time!"

"I will free Mr.
Nuggy if you can get
me what I want."

"Yes, anything," I
say.

"I want a princess."

"A *princess*? Where am I going to get a . . ."
And then I look over at Rosabelle, cutting her
grapes in half and eating them with a fork.

I do some quick math in my head.

the poufy dresses + the crown + the high heels +

the tea set + the dragon + the castle +

the earrings + cutting her grapes =

"No problem!" I say, smiling, because I'm certain that *Rosabelle is going to love this game!* I hang up. "Meet me on the playground," I say to Rosabelle in my dead serious voice. "You're in danger and it's top secret."

"Really?" she says, her eyes suddenly lit up like fireworks. She quickly packs up her lunch and I can barely keep up with her out the door to the playground.

Rosabelle screams SOOOOO LOUD when I tell her about Mrs. Gobble Gracker that the hopscotch girls cover their ears and run away.

"Tell me everything," says Rosabelle. "And I mean *everything*."

"Well, she has pointy teeth, a black cape, a long nose, sharp black nails, crooked shoes, a creepy bun . . .

Rosabelle walks back and forth, thinking. She looks very serious. For a long time, she doesn't say anything.

Finally, she opens her mouth to speak.

"We'll have to go to war," she says.

"*War???*" I say.

"Do you have a horse?"

"Um . . . "

"*You need a horse!* We have to be prepared to fight. This war isn't just about us. This is about protecting the whole kingdom. Who else is on Mrs. Gobble Gracker's side?"

"I don't think anybody. . . . I've never seen anyone else but . . . "

"She is definitely not working alone! I'm sure she has helpers. How many prisoners has she already taken? And where are they all?" asks Rosabelle.

"Um . . . um . . . I don't know . . . ," I say. "I never thought about it. She has a cave."

"*You never thought about it??*" Rosabelle

gasps. "This is about injustice! We'll have to free them! I bet her cave is *full* of prisoners! It's up to US to save them! We need a plan. *A real plan*. We can't take any risks. I'm not going to spend the rest of my life spinning gold in a cave, or whatever!"

Then she starts talking even faster. "It's too bad my dragon is so injured right now, but I can gather some knights when I get home from school . . .

"and we need to make
a map of the woods
to locate her cave,

and I'll get my horse . . .

and see if I can find my
sword . . . and . . .

. . . and . . . lemon juice!"
she suddenly shouts. "We'll
need your lemon juice!"

And then recess is over.

That afternoon during math time, I whisper to Rosabelle, "There's one more thing I have to tell you. I have a fairy godmother named Mr. Nuggy, and he accidentally turned into a chicken."

"Oh! That same thing happened to my fairy godmother once!" whispers Rosabelle.

"Hey! What are you guys talking about?" asks George. "Chicken? Raise your hand if you love chicken!"

That night at dinner, my dad asks me, "Dory, what happened at school today?"

"Rosabelle and I planned a war!" I shout.

"Thank God it's Friday," says my mom.

Friday Night

Peter Pan hat

my goggles

Captain America Shield

Horsey

flashlight and large fork

backpack full of bananas

Luke's army pants

MARY, READY FOR WAR

CHAPTER 6
In the Woods

It's Saturday morning and I just want to stay home in my nightgown, but my dad drags us to the park.

As soon as we get there, I hang on my dad and whine, "Can we go home now?"

"No," he says. "Go play."

Instead, I ask him questions. Any question I can think of.

"Can't you just go on the swings?" asks my dad.

I wait for the swings. And wait. And wait.
And wait. Every time I'm about to get a swing,
a big kid races up and gets it before me.

Ugh! Big kids.

I guess I'll go dig in
the sandbox. But right
away I dig to the bottom.
I hit wood. "I guess there's
nowhere left to go," I
grumble.

Next, I try to go down the slide, but this giant toddler with a gross runny nose keeps running up the slide.

"Can you move, please?" I ask him a million times. "MOVE! Or you are going to get hit when I go down!"

After a couple of times crashing into him face-to-face, I worry that I could catch his runny nose. Yuck. Forget this slide.

Luke is running around chasing pigeons with a stick. And Violet is with her friends. Violet always has friends at the park.

"*Now* can we go home?" I ask my dad. But he's reading a book and not listening to me.

That's when I see a chicken over there by that tree. I crawl to the other side of the bench to get a better look.

"Hey, Dad, I'm going to play right near those trees over there," I say.

"Okay," he says. "Don't go too far."

I'm really good at pretending I'm far away, when I'm not.

"Mr. Nuggy! Are you okay?" I say, picking up the chicken and kissing him. *He's soooooo cute as a chicken!*

"Bok!" he says.

"How did you get free?" I ask. But it's true, all he can do is bok.

"How do I turn you back into my fairy godmother?"

"Bok! Bok!"

"Right! You need your magic wand! Where is it?"

He points deep into the woods.

"Okay," I say, "let's go find it."

We walk through the woods for hours.

117

Along the way,
many animals
stop to greet us.

Then I see a mysterious girl coming toward me through the woods. She is wearing a long fancy dress with a tall pointy hat with ribbons hanging down. As she gets closer, I see that she is carrying a wooden sword and eating an apple.

It's Rosabelle.

When she sees me, she smiles for a second and then she starts screaming, "Help! Help! This apple is poisonous. I'm slowly dying!" And then she falls to the ground.

"I'm dying, I'm dying," she says, and makes lots of creepy dying sounds. "Uuugg-hhhh, Eeee-uuu . . ."

"Who gave you the apple?" I ask.

"Kkk-hhhhhggg . . . a very old woman," she says in a weak voice I can barely hear. Her eyes are closed.

"What did she look like?" I ask.

"She had a black bun, a big collar, and evil eyebrows. She had teeth as sharp as scissors . . . a nose as long as a broomstick . . . a cape as dark as midnight."

I try to imagine who this could be.

And then I realize, "Stupid me! You mean *Mrs. Gobble Gracker!*"

"Yes, her," Rosabelle says. "I was on my way to my cottage in the woods, and my dragon was so tired he fell asleep under a tree, and I was all alone, and suddenly I was caught in this big horrible net! Mrs. Gobble Gracker's trap!"

"Of course!" I say, remembering that Mrs. Gobble Gracker wanted a princess. "She captured you! That explains why she freed Mr. Nuggy!"

"Anyway," says Rosabelle, "she seemed a little nice at first, because she offered me this apple. It looked so red and juicy, but as soon as I took a tiny bite, I started to feel my ears getting hot, my toes very itchy, and my heart was *sweating*! And I knew right away that I WAS DYING."

"Wow! Mrs. Gobble Gracker is deadlier than I thought!" I say. "How did she make a poison apple spell?"

That's when Mr. Nuggy starts bokking his head off, flapping his wings, and getting all big and puffy. He is trying to tell me something.

He boks so hard he actually throws up.

Poor guy.

BOK!
BOK! BOK!
BOK! BOK!
BOK! BOK!
BOK! BOK!
BOK! BOK!

1.   2.   3.

And then I suddenly figure out what he is trying to tell me.

"Because she stole your magic wand! That's how!!" I yell.

"BOK!" he says, jumping back onto his feet.

"How did she get your wand?" I ask.

"Bok! Bok!"

"Because you're a chicken and you have no hands or cool belt holder anymore?"

"BOK!"

"Awwww, it's okay. I'll get it back," I say petting him.

"Come on, we've got to go," I tell Rosabelle. "I can reverse the spell, but I'll need the magic wand. And the only way to get it is to battle Mrs. Gobble Gracker for it. We've got to find her cave!"

In her weak voice, Rosabelle says, "We don't have a lot of time."

"I know you're dying, but can you get up?"

"Can you come with me? Can you walk a little?"

"Just a little," she says, barely able to breathe.

And that's when we discover Mrs. Gobble Gracker's footprints.

CHAPTER 7
Launched into Battle

We follow Mrs. Gobble Gracker's pointy footprints into a creepy bat cave, through a giant spiderweb, and into a thick dark forest....

I clear a path through the forest by
chopping down little trees and branches
with Rosabelle's sword.

On the other side of the forest, we find Mrs. Gobble Gracker sitting by a fire. From behind the bushes, Rosabelle waves quietly to the prisoners who are peeking out of the cave.

"What should we do now?" I whisper to Rosabelle.

"Well, I'm dying," she whispers. "So, YOU jump out with the sword."

"I need to look scary," I say.

"That's easy," she says.

Behind the bushes, Rosabelle rubs some mud on my face and arms.

"How about this?" I whisper, putting my shirt over my head, which makes my hair stick straight up.

"How about this?" she says, and then mushes up my hair even more and throws a bunch of pine needles in it.

"Now you look like a super freak!" she laughs. "Come here, I'll launch you."

I've never been launched before!

"Wait. Just in case we need it, I've got lemon juice," Rosabelle says.

Then she ducks down low and pushes me in the butt, hard.

I'M LAUNCHED!

I land on my feet.

"Dory?" says Mrs. Gobble
Gracker. "Is that you?"

"Nope," I say, shaking
my head. "Not me."

I forgot how easy
it is to trick her.

"Well, whoever you are, did you come for Violet's doll?"

"Nobody cares about that doll anymore. Not even Violet. I came for the wand," I say.

"Ha-ha! Good luck with that!" she says.

Mrs. Gobble Gracker pulls out her own sword. Bigger, shinier, and sharper.

But with one ninja slash from me, and a squirt of lemon juice in the eye from Rosabelle, Mrs. Gobble Gracker is blinded and her cape catches on fire.

"Remember when I asked you
if she has helpers?" says Rosabelle,
clenching her teeth.

Ouch,
Ouch!

Rosabelle's dragon leads the knights to our rescue and together we fight a wild and crazy battle.

And lose.

But nobody thought to tie up a chicken.

Mr. Nuggy runs into the cave ...

grabs the wand and . . .

chicken no more.

Mr. Nuggy quickly unties us and then frees the prisoners.

After our escape, everyone runs home, except us. Now that Mr. Nuggy is finally back to himself, we laugh really hard that he was a chicken. Hilarious!

Then Mr. Nuggy reverses Rosabelle's poison spell.

"Now hop around on one foot, and sneeze two times, and bend your elbows back like this," he tells her.

"How can I hop around on one foot when I'm dying? Okay, fine!" says Rosabelle. "And by the way, nice hat."

"You too," he says.

As soon as the spell is reversed, Rosabelle says, "Uh-oh. Did you hear a noise? Listen!"

I hear Violet calling me from the playground. "Rascal! Come on! We're leaving! It's starting to rain."

"Oh no!" I say. "I wish we were still tied up."

"I know," says Rosabelle, wiping dirt off my face. "But we better go."

We say good-bye to Mr. Nuggy, since he lives in the woods anyway. Before he leaves, he whispers to me, "The pancake recipe was too complicated. I can't . . ."

"It's okay," I say. "School's not THAT bad."

"It was nice to meet you," Rosabelle says to Mr. Nuggy.

Rosabelle and I walk back into the playground.

"This is my best friend, Rosabelle," I say, introducing her to Luke and Violet.

Their mouths drop open in disbelief.

"Huh???" says Luke.

"*Rosabelle??*" says Violet.

"Rosabelle, come on! We're leaving, too."

"I'm coming, Daddy!" calls Rosabelle.

Her dad definitely does not look like a king.

Ta-ta!

"Bye, Rascal!" waves Rosabelle. "See you on Monday!!"

Luke and Violet stare at Rosabelle as she walks off holding her daddy's hand.

Then they look at me.

"Told you," I say.

"And then what happened?" asks Mary.

"After the princess was saved from Mrs. Gobble Gracker's spell, all the creatures in the woods cheered with joy," I say. "The prisoners went home to their mushroom houses. The woods was a peaceful place again. And I was a hero."

"Wow! Tell it again," says Mary.

The End

Abby Hanlon (www.abbyhanlon.com) is a former teacher. Inspired by her students' storytelling, she began to write her own stories for children, and taught herself to draw. She is the author of *Ralph Tells a Story* and the Dory Fantasmagory series. The first, *Dory Fantasmagory*, was an ALA Notable Book, a *Kirkus*, *Publishers Weekly*, and *Parent's* Magazine Best Book, and a Golden Kite Honor Book. The second, *The Real True Friend*, won a Cybil Award, and the third, *Dory Dory Black Sheep*, was an ALA Notable Book. Abby lives in Brooklyn, New York, with her husband and their two children.

Good-bye!

Good-bye!

The End

(Yes, really!)